Peas in a Pod

www.kidsatrandomhouse.co.uk

Peas in a Pod

Adèle Geras

Illustrated by Peter Bailey

For Sophie and Stephanie Pitt

PEAS IN A POD
A CORGI PUPS BOOK

First publication in Great Britain

PRINTING HISTORY
Corgi Pups edition published 2000

ISBN 0 552 54947 9

Set in 18/25pt Bembo Schoolbook by
Phoenix Typesetting, Ilkley, West Yorkshire

Corgi Pups Books are published by Transworld Publishers,
61-63 Uxbridge Road, Ealing, London W5 5SA,
a division of the Random House Group Ltd,
in Australia by Random House Australia (Pty) Ltd,
20 Alfred Street, Milsons Point, Sydney, NSW 2061, Australia
in New Zealand by Random House New Zealand Ltd,
18 Poland Road, Glenfield, Auckland 10, New Zealand
and in South Africa by Random House (Pty) Ltd,
Endulini, 5a Jubilee Road, Parktown 2193, South Africa

Printed and bound in Denmark by
Nørhaven Paperback, Viborg

Contents

Series Reading Consultant: Prue Goodwin
Reading and Language Information Centre,
University of Reading

Chapter One

When Stella-across-the-road decided to get married, Jo was very happy. "I bet she asks us to be her bridesmaids," she told her sister Lily.

"She's been our babysitter for years and years, so we're practically family. We'll have really beautiful clothes to wear. I can't wait."

Lily sniffed, and didn't look happy at all. "I don't want to be a bridesmaid. Maybe she'll decide she only wants one bridesmaid, and then she's sure to choose you."

Jo was nine years old. She was
small and thin. Lily was seven
and tall for her age. Sometimes,
when they were dressed alike,
people thought they might be
twins, and this made Jo cross,

 because she hated being the same size as someone who was two years younger. Lily hated putting on dresses or skirts and spent most of her time wearing jeans. Jo wanted to be a ballerina when she grew up but, for the moment, being a bridesmaid was one of her main ambitions.

Michelle, her friend, had been
one last year, and Jo felt very
envious. Now maybe her dream
was going to come true.

Jo drew pictures of pretty bridesmaids on every spare piece of paper she could find. Some had ribbons in their hair, some had flowers all over their dresses, but all the skirts were long and puffed-out. Jo thought they were lovely.

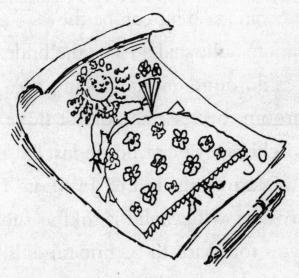

Sometimes she made Lily play weddings. "You can be the groom," she said. "I'll be the bride."

Lily quite enjoyed being the groom, because she didn't have to change out of her jeans.

Every night in bed Jo said: "I wonder why Stella is taking such ages to ask us to be bridesmaids."

"I don't know," said Lily. "Don't worry about it. Go to sleep."

But Jo did worry about it.

The next day she made Lily play hopscotch with her outside Stella's house.

"Hello, girls," said Stella when she came down the road on her way back from work. "Are you looking forward to my wedding? I've got to write the invitations tonight." She went in without saying a word about bridesmaids.

"We'll come back again tomorrow," Jo said. "If she keeps seeing us, she'll remember in the end that she hasn't asked us yet."

After two weeks of hanging about outside Stella's house, Lily and Jo gave up. Stella's mum, Mrs Grainger, had chatted to them about flower arrangements; Stella's granny had asked them in for a drink and a biscuit, and shown them a picture of what the wedding cake was going to

look like. No-one had even
mentioned bridesmaids.

"Maybe," said Lily, "she's not
going to have any."

That was such an awful thing
to say that Jo decided to pretend
she hadn't heard it.

Chapter Two

Then one day Stella's mum came in to have a cup of coffee with Lily and Jo's mum. "Wedding day's nearly here," she said. "Aren't you getting excited, girls?"

Jo opened her mouth to ask about the bridesmaids, but Mrs Grainger just kept on talking.

"It's going to be a wedding to remember," she told them. "Three bridesmaids and two pages – that's Stella's cousins and her niece and nephews – and the best man and me and Stella's dad and granny.

It's going to be quite a crowd but just wait till you hear where they're having the wedding – in the Rose Garden at Hatton Hall. You know, that stately home just outside town. Stella's gran thinks it's a shame not to have a wedding in a church, or at least a Registry Office, but everyone has to do what will make them happy. That's what I think."

Lily was just going to ask
what happened if it rained,
when Mrs Grainger said, as
though she had been reading
Lily's mind: "And if it rains,
there's a lovely big drawing
room they use for the weddings."

Jo wasn't really listening. She was too upset. She wasn't going to be a bridesmaid after all. It isn't fair, she said to herself.

She blinked very quickly, because she felt like crying, but she was going to wait till she and Lily were alone to do that. This was easily the saddest day of her whole life.

After Mrs Grainger had finished telling them how grand the wedding was going to be, she said goodbye and went home.

"I hope it pours with rain!" Jo shouted after her. "I hope they have a horrible wedding. I hope the wedding cake tastes awful!"

"Jo!" said Mum. "What's the matter with you? Why are you behaving like a little monster?"

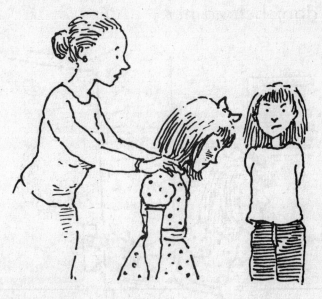

"She thought we were going to be bridesmaids," Lily explained. "And we're not, so now she's fed up. I'm not fed up. I'm glad."

"Then you're a silly little brat!" Jo shouted and left the room in a temper, slamming the door behind her.

"Oh dear," said Mum. "I was just about to tell her that I'm going to buy lovely dresses for you both to wear. I'll go after her and try to cheer her up." She ran upstairs after Jo.

It was Lily's turn to look glum. She didn't want a lovely

dress. She wanted a new pair of trainers with silver stripes on them.

Chapter Three

On the morning
of Stella's
wedding day
Jo was ready
straight after
breakfast, but

Lily was taking
ages to put on
last year's party
frock. She'd
refused to wear
anything like
Jo's new dress.

"Come on, Lily!" Jo called out. "It's time to go over now and see Stella's dress and meet the bridesmaids."

She looked out of the window.

The sun was trying to shine,
but clouds were rushing across
the sky, and sometimes they
became dark and heavy and
rain started falling, blown about
by a strong wind. She wondered
if she had made the bad weather
appear by wishing for it. Maybe

Stella would have to get married indoors after all. Her veil would be blown about all over the place. The hem of her dress and her train might drag in a puddle and get all muddy.

"Right," said Lily, coming into the room. "I'm ready now."

"We're going then, Mum," said Jo. "Is that OK?"

"Be back here by half past," said Mum. "We're getting a lift down to Hatton Hall with Stella's Uncle Archie. Just wait for this shower to be over."

"Why are you still looking cross?" Lily asked Jo. "I'm the one who should be cross. I hate this dress. I look stupid. You like yours, I know you do."

Jo didn't answer straight away. She *did* like her dress, which was pink and lacy with a wide velvet sash for a belt. Mum had bought a special matching velvet ribbon for her hair. She knew she looked pretty, but still . . .

"I wanted to go in a shiny car," she said to Lily. "And the bridesmaids have got baskets to carry. With real flowers in them."

"Stella's got to choose her relations first," Lily said.

"I know," said Jo, "but she could have had us as well."

"Then the whole garden would be full of bridesmaids," said Lily. "It'd look silly."

"It wouldn't," said Jo.

"Would," said Lily.

"Stop squabbling, girls," said
Mum, "and go across the road.
It's very kind of the Graingers to
invite you. They must be run off
their feet."

The Graingers' house was so full
of people that Lily and Jo could
hardly find a
corner to stand
in. Stella's
granny was
trying to see
herself in the
hall mirror, Mrs Grainger was

running up
and down
stairs,
fetching this
and that for the
bride, Mr Grainger
was mumbling in the kitchen,

 practising his speech, and Pepper, Stella's little brown and white dog, was racing from room to room. Every now and then he stopped in the middle of the carpet and began chasing his own tail.

"Come with me, girls," said Mrs Grainger. She was already dressed for the wedding, but still had rollers in her hair.

"What if she forgets?" Lily asked Jo in a whisper. "Imagine how funny that'd be!"

"Ssh," said Jo. "She'll hear you."

Mrs Grainger opened Stella's bedroom door and Lily and Jo went in.

"Oooh!" said Jo. She wanted to say so many things, and couldn't think of one of them. Stella looked just like a princess. Her hair was done up in an enormous

heap of curls on top of her head.
Her dress was made of satin. There
were tiny pearls scattered all over
the bodice in flower patterns.

"You look beautiful," said Lily.
"Really, truly beautiful."

"I was going to say that," said
Jo crossly.

Stella smiled at them both. "So do you," she said, and then she made a funny face, pretending to be scared. "But I'm feeling a bit nervous. Something's bound to go wrong."

"No, it won't," said Jo. "Everything will be perfect."

"Now, Lily and Jo," said Stella. "I'd like you to meet my bridesmaids – Ruthie, Bridie and little Amee."

"Hello," said Lily.

"Hello," said Jo.

"Hello," said Ruthie, who was the eldest. "We've been told to sit as quiet as mice, and not move, in case our dresses get dirty."

The bridesmaids were wearing pale blue silky dresses.

They had white rosebuds pinned into their hair. Jo was just thinking how lovely they looked and feeling sad all over again at not being a bridesmaid, when they heard it. Mrs Grainger was shrieking in the hall. What on earth had happened?

Chapter Four

Jo and Lily ran downstairs. Stella's mum was standing by the front door talking to her daughter-in-law Margie who was all dressed up in her wedding clothes.

"Why didn't you tell me earlier?" she wailed. "I could have done something. And what about poor little Matt and Peter? Who's going to look after them? Your next-door neighbour? Well, I don't know what to say, I really don't."

"Come on now, dearest," said Mr Grainger. "What's the problem?"

"Those two scallywags have only chosen today to break out in German measles, that's what," said Stella's mum.

"And here's Margie with their clothes in a parcel. As if I could find two pages at a moment's notice! I ask you!"

"I must go," said Margie. "I promised the boys I'd get out a video for them before we leave for the wedding." She was gone, and Mr Grainger closed the door behind her.

By now, even Stella had come to see what was going on. "Let's go and sit down," she said. "There's nothing to worry about. I've got three bridesmaids after all."

"I spent a fortune on those pages' suits," Mrs Grainger sniffed. "What a waste!"

"Two pairs of blue velvet trousers," said Stella, laying them carefully on the back of the sofa. "Two white silk shirts. Two pairs of black shoes with silver buckles. And two gorgeous silver brocade waistcoats."

The Grainger family gathered round the sofa and sighed over the clothes. Granny Grainger put her glasses on and stared at Lily and Jo. "I've had an idea," she said.

"Later, Mother, dear," said Mrs

Grainger. "You can tell us later. We've got to get going now. The cars will be here in half an hour."

"Later will be too late," said Granny Grainger. "I've solved the problem. I've found you two pages."

"Where?" said Stella, and all the Graingers looked around as though pages might have been hiding somewhere in their lounge.

Granny Grainger pointed at
Lily and Jo. "There," she said.

"But they're girls, Granny," said
Stella. "How can you have girl
pages?"

"I don't see why not. Don't call
them pages, that's all. Call them
. . . I don't know . . . attendants.
That's it. Wedding attendants."

Everyone was quiet for a
moment, then Stella said, "It
might work . . . what do you
think, Lily? And you, Jo? I never

realized how alike you two were.
Just like two peas in a pod, you'd
be, if you wore matching suits.
How do you feel about standing
in for the boys? You're very
important, you know. You have to
carry the bridal train. Do you
think you could manage that?"

 "Oh, yes," said Jo. "But will the clothes fit us?"

"Nothing a safety pin or two won't be able to fix," said Granny.

"Go and try them on," said Mrs Grainger, "while I run across and warn your mum that you might be coming with us in the wedding party."

Chapter Five

Lily and Jo stared at their reflections in Stella's long mirror.

"Well," said Mrs Grainger. "A bit of a rush job but, though I say it myself, you both look wonderful."

"Brilliant!" Lily agreed. "I pretend to be a boy all the time

anyway, so I'm really good at it. People might think I'm a real boy, mightn't they?"

"Course they won't," said Jo. "You've got girls' black shoes on, haven't you?"

"It doesn't matter at all," said Stella. "We're lucky that the shoes were the only things that didn't really fit."

Jo didn't know if she was pleased or not. She would be riding in a shiny car. She would have her photo in the wedding

album. She and Lily would be
Very Important and everyone
would look at them, and say
how good it was of them to be

wedding attendants at the very
last minute. All that was going to
be like a dream come true, but
there was a tiny part of Jo that
was sorry she'd had to take off
her own lovely pink dress and
scrape her hair back into a tight
bun, and leave her velvet hair
ribbon at home.

And however smart she and Lily looked, they still wouldn't have long skirts, and baskets full of flowers to carry. Jo and Lily were in the second car, with Mrs Grainger and Granny Grainger. It was shiny, but not as big as the bride's car. That was white and there were white ribbons tied to the bonnet, and lots of white flowers piled up against the back window. Stella and her dad were going to the wedding in it, and so were the bridesmaids.

The rain was coming down very heavily. Stella came out of the front door with her satin skirt pulled up so that it didn't get wet and dirty. Mr Grainger was holding an umbrella over her and looking worried.

It was quite a long ride to Hatton Hall. The rain splashed against the windscreen. Jo whispered to Lily: "It's my fault."

"What is?"

"This rain," Jo said.

"Don't you remember? I wished Stella would have a rainy wedding day. Now we'll have to be indoors."

"That's stupid," said Lily. "It's not raining because you wished it. And anyway, it's stopped. Look."

There wasn't time to look.

They had arrived. Stella was standing on the steps of the Hall, looking like a white flower. There was her groom and the best man, and Ruthie, Bridie and Amee, holding tight to their baskets of white flowers. Lily and Jo went up the steps and the best man showed them where they had to stand.

"These," Stella said to everyone, "are my wedding attendants. They've taken over from Matt and Peter at very short notice. They're both real stars. Thank you, Jo and Lily!"

"You look brilliant," Ruthie whispered. "And you've got something proper to do, holding up Stella's train. We can't do anything with these flowers to carry."

"But won't the hem of the dress get muddy?" Jo asked. "No," Bridie said. "They've put down a red carpet. Look."

Mrs Grainger showed Lily and Jo how to hold the train, and everyone set off for the Rose Garden, where all the guests were waiting for Stella and her bridesmaids to arrive.

"There are the pages," someone said. "They look quite splendid, don't they?"

Everyone clapped. Jo whispered to Lily: "I like being a wedding attendant. I don't even mind not having a basket of flowers." The sun shone down and made everything sparkle. Lily pulled her shoulders back and walked carefully along the red carpet, and Jo smiled at her, feeling happy that she was part of such a special wedding day.

THE END